Also by Becky Bloom and Pascal Biet
Mice Make Trouble
Wolf!

*To the children of Fawcett School,
Cambridge*
—B.B. and P.B.

Copyright © 2000 by Siphano Picture Books
First American edition 2001 published by Orchard Books
First published in the United Kingdom in 2000 by Siphano Picture Books Ltd. under the title *Biscuit*

All rights reserved. No part of this book may be reproduced or transmitted in any form or by any means, electronic or mechanical, including photocopying, recording, or by any information storage or retrieval system, without permission in writing from the Publisher.

Orchard Books, an imprint of Scholastic Inc., 95 Madison Avenue, New York, NY 10016

Printed and bound by Phoenix Color Corp. The text of this book is set in 18 point Caslon 224 Book. The illustrations are watercolor.
10 9 8 7 6 5 4 3 2 1

Library of Congress Cataloging-in-Publication Data
Bloom, Becky.
Crackers / by Becky Bloom ; illustrated by Pascal Biet.—lst American ed.
p.   cm.
Summary: Crackers the cat has trouble keeping a job until he finds one that is perfect for him.
ISBN 0-531-30326-8 (alk. paper)
[1. Cats—Fiction. 2. Work—Fiction. 3. Mice—Fiction.] I. Biet, Pascal, ill. II. Title.
PZ7.B62275 Cr 2001 [E]—dc21 00-55778

Crackers

by **Becky Bloom**

illustrated by **Pascal Biet**

ORCHARD BOOKS   NEW YORK
An Imprint of Scholastic Inc.

One morning Crackers the cat came back from his daily jog and sat down for breakfast. He opened the newspaper and turned to the want ads.

"Today I am going to find a job," he declared.

WANTED:
SECURITY GUARD
FOR WAREHOUSE.
MUST BE BIG,
STRONG, AND
TOUGH-LOOKING.

"That sounds interesting," said Crackers. "I'm big, for a cat, and quite strong, and I can look tough if I really want to." He put on clothes to make him look extra tough, and off he went to the warehouse.

"The job is yours," said the warehouse owner, a big bulldog. "We need a tough cat like you around here."

All went well . . . until Crackers gave some
scrap wood to a handy mouse who came by.
The bulldog got very angry. "Why do you
think I hired a cat in the first place!" he shouted.
"You're supposed to chase mice in this
warehouse, not make friends with them.
Now beat it— and don't set foot
in here again!"

Crackers went back to his newspaper and found another advertisement.

WANTED:

ASSISTANT FOR PLEASURE BOAT RENTALS, RIVERSIDE MARINA. MUST SWIM AND ROW. LIFESAVING SKILLS HELPFUL.

Crackers was a good swimmer and had once been a lifeguard at the local kitty pool. He put on clothes to give him an extra sporty look, and off he went to the riverside marina.

"Congratulations—you've got the job," said the owner, a beaver. He showed Crackers around the docks. "We can use a cat with your skills."

All went well . . . until Crackers let a family of mice fish from the pier. The customers who rented pleasure boats didn't like mice and complained to the beaver.

"It's that cat's fault!" Crackers heard the beaver say. Crackers left before the beaver could yell at him.

"I'm not having much luck," said Crackers. Then he remembered another advertisement in the newspaper.

WANTED:
WAITER FOR NEW
RESTAURANT.
MUST BE PRESENTABLE,
WITH GOOD MANNERS.
KNOWLEDGE OF FRENCH ESSENTIAL.

"Perfect!" exclaimed Crackers. He had taken French in school. He put on clothes to make him look dapper, and off he went to the restaurant.

"Congratulations!" said the headwaiter, a duck. "You're the ideal cat for the job."

All went well . . . until a couple of mice came into the restaurant. Crackers ushered them to the center table.

"Mice! Mice!" shrieked the ducks, jumping out of their seats.

"Mice in the restaurant!" squawked a chicken, flapping her wings.

Crackers didn't even wait for the feathers to clear. He just slipped quietly out the back door.

"It seems that bosses who hire cats only want them to chase mice," said Crackers sadly. "But I don't want to chase mice. After all, they never chase me!"

Just then he saw a sign in a store window.

SQUEAK & COMPANY CHEESE SHOP
WANTED: ASSISTANT

"I'd really like that job," sighed Crackers, "but mice would never hire a cat."

Crackers couldn't stop thinking about the cheese shop. Maybe if he didn't look too catty, they might consider him for the job!

He tried on all kinds of clothes and disguises, but no matter what he wore, he still looked like a cat.

Suddenly he had an idea. "Perhaps the mice I've met will help me."

And off he ran to find them.

The mice were delighted to see Crackers again.

"Of course we'll help you," they said. "We'll go to the cheese shop right away and have a word with the manager."

And they did.

"This cat gave me the scrap wood I needed to finish my den," said the handy mouse.

"He let us fish from the pier, and we caught a huge guppy!" said the mice children.

"He gave us the best table at Chez Canard," added the mouse couple.

"Well . . . ," said the cheese shop manager, eyeing Crackers reluctantly. "All right, I'll give you a try." And he shook hands with Crackers.

Soon Crackers was the most famous cat in town. Mice came from far and wide just to buy cheese from him and shake his hand.

The manager of Squeak & Company Cheese Shop couldn't have been more pleased.

Best of all, Crackers was never fired again! "I always thought I belonged in a cheese shop," he said happily.